F L

FLY

ALISON HUGHES

Kids Can Press

Published in Canada and the U.S. by Kids Can Press Ltd.
25 Dockside Drive, Toronto, ON M5A 0B5

Kids Can Press is a Corus Entertainment Inc. company

www.kidscanpress.com

The text is set in Crimson Text.

Edited by Sarah Harvey
Designed by Andrew Dupuis
Cover illustration by Andrew Dupuis

Printed and bound in Shenzhen, China, in 3/2022 by C & C Offset

CM 22 0 9 8 7 6 5 4 3 2 1

FSC
www.fsc.org
MIX
Paper from
responsible sources
FSC® C008047

Library and Archives Canada Cataloguing in Publication

Title: Fly / written by Alison Hughes.
Names: Hughes, Alison, 1966– author.
Identifiers: Canadiana 2021034234X | ISBN 9781525305832 (hardcover)
Classification: LCC PS8615.U3165 F59 2022 | DDC jC813/.6 — dc23

Kids Can Press gratefully acknowledges that the land on which our office is located is the traditional territory of many nations, including the Mississaugas of the Credit, the Anishnabeg, the Chippewa, the Haudenosaunee and the Wendat peoples, and is now home to many diverse First Nations, Inuit and Métis peoples.

We thank the Government of Ontario, through Ontario Creates; the Ontario Arts Council; the Canada Council for the Arts; and the Government of Canada for supporting our publishing activity.

For Ben — A.H.

THE SLIDE OF STEEL

"En garde!"
A hoarse cry
muffled by a mesh mask,
and the
combatants
raise their swords
and freeze —
coiled,
       tense,
              waiting,
                     ready.

"Allez!"
They spring into action
and my blood
leaps with them.
Quick steps
pacing
                     forward
       back
stealthy as
predators.
A measured retreat,
          a vicious   *t h r u s t,*
a parry,
the clash of steel,
once,
twice,
then
a long,
       sliding,
             blade-on-blade
                  h i s s s s.

They step   apart,
        thinking,
        planning,
        assessing,
        alert.
They thrum
in stillness
and
        I
                hold
                my
                breath.

Then:
                                prod
                clink
deflect
                                advance
                clank
parry
                                quickstep
retreat,
back and forth
until a final, springing
                                l u n g e!
Lightning quick,
straight to the heart.
No blood,
but what drama,
what tragedy
is released in that
final act!

MERE MORTALS

The spell breaks.
The demo's over,
and the watching
class
erupts in
applause
that
echoes off
the gym walls.

The faux combatants
push up
grilled masks,
faces flushed,
hair damp.
An average woman,
an average man.
Olympians
(with medals to prove it),
but mere mortals
after all.
The magic dissipates,
evaporates,
as they ruin the duel
by explaining it.

"Everyone'll get a turn with the gear,"
she says.

"And remember,
in fencing
movement and quick thinking

                                        can overcome
                                        height,
                                        reach
                                        or strength."
She glances uneasily at me,
seeing
obvious obstacles
that can't be overcome.

What does she see
when she looks at me?
From fourteen years'
experience
of gawkers,
I can guess.
First: my wheelchair
(my most distinctive feature
to the un-wheeled).
Eyes often
                        slide   away
after that first glance
like I'm a book
clapped
          shut.

Next up:
my body.
Slight,
gangly —
arms and legs,
hands and fingers
flex-locked in
          cramped
                    crumpled
          contortions.

She hasn't turned
away yet,
like so many
others who —
perturbed,
disturbed —
display the
uneasy
squeamishness
of the supposedly
"normal."

Last: my face.
Less alarming —
a fine face
(despite clenched teeth
and a problematic
tongue).
Dark hair
that can't be tamed,
a nose I wish was smaller
(does anybody love their nose?)
and glasses framing
                              shrewd,
                sharp
brown eyes.
She looks into them
and, briefly,
two mortals
meet.

I'm the first
to look away.
I salute her for
persevering
all the way to the eyes,

                    but   reject,
                                    deflect,
                    parry
her pity
by denying
her
my rare smile.

HIDDEN KNIGHTS

Two boys suit up,
and the rest of the class
practices
fencing footwork by
flailing badminton rackets,
woeful substitutes for
lethal sabers.

I'm done here.
I gave up computer time
to feel the thrill of battle
at the only interesting gym class
of the year.
"Bus time. Let's go, Levi," I say,
my dependable left hand
steering my chair,
veering
toward the exit.
But he lingers
and I see
that even though his job is me,
he'd have liked a turn at swordplay,
the chance to be a knight.

Even though my sword
and shield are
invisible,
I would, too.
And —
      full disclosure,
              running with the knight theme —

it's not a stretch
to say
that
I have a quest,
a trusty steed,
a damsel in distress
and a
villain
to prove it.

ESCAPE

"Got everything?"

Levi asks
at the bus stop,
checking my backpack
before he tucks it
behind me.

"Want that jacket on?"

"I'm good. You go,"
I say,
waving my aide
away.

"You're the boss!"

He smiles,
waves
and slips away
into the crowd.

When I know
I'm alone,
I whisper
"En garde!"
in elegant (yet
clenched) French,
my hand closing on
a sleek, imaginary sword.
And, as if it senses
my shifting grip,
my jacket seizes its chance
and slips
    into the
        buffeting
            wind.

Allez!

I snatch at it
in desperation,
frustration,
but grasp only air.
It's off —
tumbling and skidding,
waving its arms wildly,
giddy with
its first taste of freedom.
    Going,
              going,
                           gone.

Helpless,
I watch it loop past the school,
                twirling,
     whirling,
              dancing
                     along the ground
until it
    snags
on a sharp corner
and,
in another gust,
darts behind the school
to hang with the vapers,
watch the cheer team practice
out of the corners of its eyes,
or settle in a heap
to dream in the cool grass.
Total freedom.

How pathetic
is my uprush of
envy
of twenty bucks' worth
of polyester?

IMPOSSIBLE DREAM

The runaway jacket
reminds me
of my dream.
THE dream:
me (yet not me)
standing straight
and tall,
legs sturdy,
strong,
an upright man
poised
at the top of a
        steep,
           deep
              staircase
              (white marble, like in an old movie)
    spiraling down.

I breathe in,
and like the air
is helium
it
        lifts
     me
   up.
I spread my arms, and
down
    I
       fly.

Smooth, strong, perfect hand meets
smooth, strong, perfect pillar,
skimming the cold stone,

sliding round and round,
gliding down,
      down,
      endlessly
      down,
confident I can soar
up
with the slightest touch of a toe
on the
optional ground.

And dream-me wants there
to be no bottom ever,
no end to this air,
this lightness,
this weightlessness,
this freedom.
Swooping in wide circles,
there is no falling,
      no flailing,
      no panic,
      no drop.
      Not a shade of doubt.
Fearless and
controlled.
A hawk
      playing
              in
        the
              wind.

DOWN TO EARTH

My eyes still closed,
I lift my face to the
weak sun
and feel
the wind feathering
cool fingers
through my hair.
It's cold enough for that
miserable jacket
that Levi will scrounge
through the
Lost and Found
and rescue for me
tomorrow.

As I sink back to Earth
from the
soaring
memory of flight
and open my eyes,
I'm gripped with hope
that I will have the flying dream tonight.
If you stop thinking about it
right now
you just might,
says my superstitious
inner voice
as the bus lurches up,
its brakes
squealing in protest.

SO SPECIAL

"A special bus for special kids!"
Jazmin, my fourth-grade aide,
used to say that
(actually, worse, *sing* that)
daily, loudly,
unaware of this special kid's
seething
resentment.
It annoys me that,
at age fourteen,
that loathsome jingle
still runs through my head
every single time
the bus pulls up.
A special bus for special kids!
Memory
is strange:
you can
never
predict
what'll stick.

OGRE

The driver is Victor,
of course.
Always Victor.
Crabby Vic
with the bruising hands,
the smoker's breath,
the grim mouth,
and the bloodshot eyes
that never quite meet mine.

                  "C'mon, Fly, you're up,"

he grunts
impatiently,
as if *he's* been waiting for *me*,
as if he hasn't just pulled up,
as if I haven't been waiting
twenty minutes,
coatless and cold.
Without looking at me,
he lowers the lift.

FLY —
    Felix
    Landon
    Yarrow.

My name is far more
lyrical
than its insect initials.
A gentleman's name,
I would tell Crabby Vic
(if he would ever
take the time
to listen).

But Vic's job doesn't extend
to actual listening.

                       "To who? To what?"

he'd ask, astonished.

                       "To *him*?
                       Can't understand a word he says!"

No, Vic's job only includes
     hoisting up bodies in chairs,
     shoving things in backpacks (minus a coat or two),
     strapping us in too tightly, and
     driving us where we need to go.
He would
     never
think that there could
     ever
be
noble hearts and
keen minds
hidden,
sheathed like swords,
secret and unseen,
in these
problematic bodies.

FLY

Years ago,
without asking
or telling me,
my mother Sharpied
my initials on my backpack —
on the *outside* —
in ridiculously huge
                    CAPITAL LETTERS
you could see from space
in case
I ever got lost.
Totally,
utterly
enraging.
So, Felix Landon Yarrow
became, merely,
FLY,
to anyone
and everyone
in a ten-mile radius.

The nickname
spread,
and now
everybody
calls me "Fly,"
a familiarity I take exception to.
There are so many familiarities.
Too many.

But I don't say anything
as Vic casually
utters that

odious nickname.
I know the game —
Mom tells me
repeatedly:

> *Don't Make Waves.*
> *Don't Rock the Boat.*

Oddly nautical phrases,
but the indignity of it is
that I need Crabby Vic
    and his hard hands
        and his smoker's breath,
            strapping my chair in
                tight,
                    locked,
            taking a full fifty-one minutes to
    get me to my home
thirteen minutes away.

Crabby Vic and the
special bus
(*for special kids!*)
are
necessary evils
in my quest
for the
freedom
everyone else takes for granted.

AWAY AND APART

The special bus
whisks me away
from the glaring
spotlight
of the disabled parking sign
perfectly aligned
with the school's main doors,
and the
long parking spot
painted bright
disability-blue,
the stick wheelchair
looking like my white shadow.

Away we go,
from the rushing
crush,
the loud crowd of kids
released by the bell,
                              set free,
                  cut loose,
who brush past
flagpole,
bench,
garbage can,
sign
and Fly.

            Who laugh and flirt
            and herd themselves
            into babbling groups.

Who "hoard,
and sleep,
and feed,
and
    know
        not
            me"
(I read that somewhere).

MY STORY

My book was
rudely shoved
without a look
into my bag
by Crabby Vic —
jammed,
crammed between
lunch bag and
water bottle,
heedless,
careless of
potential
leaks.

Not merely a book
but a companion,
almost a friend.
Don Quixote
(the full title translates as
The Ingenious Gentleman Don Quixote of La Mancha,
which,
while it has a certain charm,
is way too long.
I call it "DQ").

It is
    famous,
    impressive,
    literary
    and very
        very
           long.

Written over four hundred years ago
when
the author,
Cervantes,
seemed to have
nothing but time
              to dream
     and ponder
              and write
                    endlessly
                         in the hot Spanish sun.

I take old
DQ everywhere,
like a good luck charm —
physical proof
to ignorant people
that there's a
mind
in this
body of mine.

Can you blame me?
So many people
make false
connections,
projections,
and assume that
because my
body malfunctions,
my mind must,
too.

This weak and faulty
logic

has followed me
like a shadow
my whole
        life
              long.

Truthfully,
even scholars agree
that
DQ's a hard read.
Maybe key
information
gets lost in translation
(like when someone
repeats
what they think
I've just said
and they're wrong).
Or maybe
you really had to be there
for the in-jokes
from the 1600s.

But I've got the gist of it
from persevering with it
(and from Wikipedia
and other media).
And say what they will
about the old knight
and his fights
("pathetic"
        "deluded"
                  "mad"
                        "sad")
at least he *tried*.

He stood alone,
unafraid
of the sharp
barbs
of criticism,
lifted his head
above life's
chaotic mess
and
sought
justice.

A quest
for a noble life:
       unsullied,
          honorable,
             pure.
A fight against
wrongs
for right —
this ideal
(more than the story itself)
appeals.
I sympathize
with old DQ:
         misunderstood,
      mocked,
    minimized.

Even saddled
with a sidekick,
he rode

alone

lone

lonely —

head held high
against the
perilous mob.

ENTERTAINMENT?

Later,
parked at home,
wheel-locked,
blocked,
trapped,
I try to read,
bracing the
balanced book,
sneaking peeks.
But it's
futile.

Long evening after
long evening,
the television blares some
moronic sitcom
at which my mother laughs,
reaching over to slap my knee
because she wants
us to be having
fun.

I smile sometimes,
which makes me
feel less mean,
more clean,
or even,
if she needs it,
crumple in a
pretend-laugh.

"Oh, I *know* it's a silly show, Felix,"
she says with a sigh.

"But this is the best part of my day,
an *escape*, in a way."

She's tired,
her back is sore,
and she deserves more
than some plastic actor
doing unrealistic things
from a badly written script.

Sadness
and sympathy
and rage
struggle inside me.
A bird
in a cage.

AWESOME

Mom's hands
are red and chapped
from the slop
she swills with a mop
over
    and over
        down her school's
            endlessly dirty
                hallways.

                "This school's a good one,"
she says.

                "The principal *thanked* me
                at the welcome assembly!
                Had me stand up while
                all the kids *clapped*!
                'Our *totally awesome* caretaker':
                that's what he called me."

But I do not trust
that word
awesome.
It's the kind of praise I get for
just showing up.
Awesome work, Felix!
The teacher's comment
on my Language Arts assignment
that was deliberate trash — a test for my teacher
to gauge exactly how
                low
her expectations of me
                could
                go.

Rock bottom,
it turns out.
She gets an F.

Awesome.
It's the kind of praise
surprised people give me
for the smallest
accomplishment
when they see
my body doesn't work
like theirs does,
and assume
my brain doesn't
work at all.

Awesome.
It's the kind of praise
you give the caretaker,
her curtain call,
before you tell her
        to get her bucket and mop
                because
                    some kid
                    puked
                        in the hall.

TOIL

My mother finally,
finally
    turns off the TV,
        tosses the remote on the couch,
    heaves a deep sigh,
        stifles a yawn.
That's the pattern.

                              "Beddy-bye, Felix,"
she says,
as if I'm two years old.
I'm not tired,
I would like to read a little more
or play a video game,
but Mom needs her sleep
and her work
isn't done
yet.

In the bathroom
she scrubs me down,
measures medicine
and wrestles me into pajamas.
I am
another heavy job
in her
long,

long

day.

If I try to help
it's worse
for both of us.
My traitor body rebels
and, for some reason,
like it has a mind of its own,
fights back.

HIDDEN DEPTHS

"Oh, my boy, my poor boy,"

she murmurs,
finally hauling me
out of my chair,
onto my bed,
breathing hard,
tucking me in.

She's called me
"my poor boy" for so long
that the phrase
is meaningless.
There's no real pity there —
it's a gust of air,
an automatic,
semi-dramatic
reflex
(like when people say
"how's it going?"
and never really mean
for you to tell them).
It used to annoy me
but doesn't anymore.
She knows I'm
more than a sigh.

As for other people,
despite the
steep,
high
walls
of sympathy they build,

the deep,
dark
wells of pity they dig,
I know one thing:

                my body is not all that I am.

I am not a poor boy.
I'm a smart one,
with talents
only a few will ever discover.
For example,
during that inane show
while other people
open-mouthed laughed,
I
blocked it out
completely.
I
sat in a
cone of perfect
silence.
I
thought of a plan
to save
Daria.

MY FAVORITE PART OF THE DAY

And now,
finally,
as I close my eyes,
I
         slip away from my body
like
         my coat in the wind,
like
         a bird on the breeze,

and
         roam
                  free.

No more
                           struggling,
            worrying,
                  fumbling,
                              flailing,
               waiting
                  or pain.

My favorite part of the day
is the night.

Maybe you'll have the flying dream,
hope whispers,
jinxing it.

TRUSTY SIDEKICK

The next morning
no sooner has Crabby Vic
lowered me down
with a clanking *thud*
from the special bus
(*for special kids!*)
than the assault
begins afresh.

"There he is!
There's the man!"

calls my aide,
weaving his way
through the jostling crowd.
Levi,
who talks too loud and
laughs too much.
Levi,
who describes himself (loudly) as

"an extra, *extra* extrovert!"

Levi,
who simply,
loudly
loves
attention.

Today he is wearing
purple pants
and a T-shirt spelling out
                Glitter-Critter
(in sparkly letters).
It suits him.

Quiet understatement
is not a phrase
in Levi's vocabulary.

He bounces
as he walks,
as if he's *just* stopping
himself from dancing.
    Which he very likely is.
        Which I appreciate —
            we hardly need to be
                even more
                ridiculously
                conspicuous.

                        "So, what's the plan, Stan?"

Levi bounces beside me as I
U-turn toward the school.
There's no real speculation;
he's making conversation.
He doesn't know
that this Stan
really *does* have a plan.

"Can you get me my book?"
I ask, then
"How are you?"
when I remember to be polite.

                        "Tired. *Dog* tired."

He hands me my book,
clamps it under my hand,
holds the door for me
and launches into a
long story about
why.

HERE'S THE LINE

Levi is a completely
wide-open book.
The opposite of
the very
closed book
that is me.

I know
> his father's girlfriend's daughter's name
> > (Cora-Lynn)
> the exact shade he painted his bedroom
> > (Hawaiian Ginger)
> his friend Konlee's "wicked" new hairstyle
> > (shaved in back, long in front)
> the disgusting carpet in his tiny apartment
> > ("putrid green")

and many,
many,
many
other Levi-things.

He knows I have cerebral palsy.
He's met my mother
(who thinks he's a "hoot").
But I haven't given him
much more than that.
Even when he asks,
> even though he's willing to listen,
> > even though I'm his first real job,
> > > even though he helps me with the most
> > > basic
> > > and intimate things.

Maybe *because* of that.

I see a line
even if he
doesn't.

DISMISSED

"Go get your coffee. Meet you in class,"
I say,
not wanting him around.
I feel exactly
as rude as I sound.
Levi's mindless chatter can
    annoy,
    irritate
    and grate
when I need to concentrate.

But rudeness
sails
over his head,
or
bounces
off the armor of his
good humor.

                    "Gotcha, gorgeous,"

he says
annoyingly,
loudly,
unprofessionally.

But at least he actually
understands me
without always asking me to
    repeat
          repeat
             always repeat.
He actually listens.
Not many people do.

He also never says:

"Are you sure?"
"Be careful."
"Can you manage?"

Or worse —
tries to help me
without asking me
first.

"Hey buddy,"

he turns and calls,

"you want anything?"

I don't,
I never do.
But I am grudgingly
pleased
that he asks.
As though he's not an aide,
as though I'm not a client.
As though we're friends.

THERE SHE IS

Rid of Levi,
I steer myself,
grateful for my steady left hand
on my chair's controller.
"The joystick," Levi calls it,
hilariously,
like I'm gaming,
rather than merely
moving.

I traverse a
wilderness
of kids
banging locker doors,
shouting to friends,
     weaving their way
         through others
       weaving the other way
           down the hall.

I roll through a
whiff of perfume,
sniff a freshly bitten
breakfast apple,
a gust of locker air,
the tang of stale sweat,
the reek of a
forgotten,
rotten
lunch.

Kids bound up the stairs
with unthinking ease
like

antelopes,
taking them two at a time, or
stand staring at their phones,
or sit on the floor,
backs propped
against lockers.

I glide by.

These things,
these people,
slide by.
All of this
is unimportant,
insignificant,
trivial.

Because there she is.

Down the hall
outside the library,
bookended by friends,
a plastic chair for
her throne.
She laughs,
her face lights up, and
              the whole
                     world
                            stills.

I drive by slowly,
straining to hear her voice
above the babble
of the crowd,
the pounding
of my
heart.

I park
close enough to see
the tilt of her head,
hear the lilt of her
laugh —
pretending to read
while I keep
watch
over
Daria.

HERS

A split-second in the fall
was all it took —
my fallen book,
her friendly look.
She picked it up,
returned it
with a smile
and
down
I
went.

A simple act
can
change a life.

                          "Don Quixote,"

she read
(pronouncing it
quick-SOTE,
which is wrong;
it's *key-HO-tay*
but I just played along).

                          "Heavy reading, hey?"

She looked right into my eyes
and smiled
a friendly smile —
not polite,
not dutiful.
No pity.
Open,
beautiful,
breathtaking.

And now I'm hers.

Her dark curls bob as she talks,
slim hands flutter to
make her point.
Smooth brown skin and sparkling eyes
and that perfect,
flashing smile.
That *smile.*
That smile that
pierces
my darkest
mood.

Her friends say

       "OMG!"

and

       "like"

every second word.
And, truthfully,
she does, too,
possibly
to fit in
or
to make them feel at ease.
But
I know,
I understand
that she is

    so

     much

      more.

THUNDER CLOUDS

A group of boys
swoops in —
                    hovering,
          circling,
                    predatory.
Obscuring my
view
of Daria.

When they think
nobody's listening,
when they think
nobody hears,
this nobody
hears.
And it's clear
that their intentions
are very
                                   far
from honorable.

One is the funny guy
("A scream!" my mother would say),
another an athlete —
push-ups in the hall
and not much
at all
in the way of brains.
But the one that comes last,
the one just stalking past,
is the real danger.
Carter.
      Who walks like he
      owns the world.

Who becomes,
effortlessly,
the center of attention
wherever he pauses.
        Who left Daria
        alone
        until recently.
                Who nobody seems
                to see through
                but
                me.

I see the girls
brighten,
straighten,
laugh louder
when Carter's near.
He pulls up a chair,
tweaks Daria's hair.
She shrugs him aside
but
(*no, no, no!*)
smiles
as she turns away.

I compose a
mental message
to Daria.
Quixote-words like
        villain
                damsel
                        chivalry
        nobility
and
                honor
flit through my mind,

but I find
ones
similarly emphatic
(but less dramatic)
that
won't make me seem
outrageously weird.

After crafting
(and rejecting)
several
mental drafts,
I settle on:

> *Carter is more dangerous*
> *than you think.*
> *I'm looking out for you.*
> *— A Friend*

THE TOLLING BELL

The merciful
bell rings, and
Daria slips away
from
Carter's
dangerous charm,
a sleek fish
fleeing a shark.

And when she is safely away,
        the crowds
    make way
for me,
too,
as I
    U-turn
        to math class
            and the
                soothing
                    simplicity
                        of numbers.

SUSTENANCE

"You don't eat enough, man,"

complains Levi.
His lively eyes are
wide and
serious,
his worry genuine.
He pushes back his
too-long, curly hair
and the single strand
he's dyed purple
escapes.

"C'mon. You gotta *eat*.
You don't eat, you *die*."

He points the banana
he's peeling at me
for emphasis.
I turn my face away
and the banana
stalls
midair.

The truth is that,
while the cafeteria
fries and gravy
smell great,
I
hate
eating in public.
The act is difficult
with an uncontrollable body,
with an unruly tongue.

Chewing and
swallowing can be
      messy,
      loud,
      undignified.
I've seen the looks I get.
I know.

Besides, it's school —
I'm not the
only one
with food issues.
Some stress-eat,
some binge and purge.
If you watch
      and listen
           like I do
               carefully
                        e n d l e s s l y
you'd be surprised
what you learn.
None of us advertise
our
problems.

A crust of bread
is all I need
anyway,
to stay vigilant
and alert
for all situations,
for any information
from the babble that
surrounds us.

"Want to talk about it?
We should *talk*."

Levi waits,
expectant,
willing me to open up,
emote,
unburden,
let him in.

And how to say,
how to convey
that I don't owe him
(or anybody)
details,
explanations
or anything at all?
     My disability,
         my difficulties,
             my pain —
often on public display —
are
in fact
all my own.
         Private.

My eyes drop,
a "Keep Out" sign
shuttering my face.
"I just want to
read my book,"
I say with
dignity.

"*Loads* of nutrition there,"

Levi says
sarcastically,
annoyingly
unimpressed.

"Betcha your crazy old knight *ate*.
Know what?
I'm gonna make you
one of my
signature smoothies,"

he threatens.

"*Mountains* of veggies.
Bright green!"

I say
"Oh, *god*"
very clearly for once,
but smile,
and Levi laughs,
delighted.

EMPTY

Two guys with trays
pause at the empty seats
beside us
in the crowded cafeteria
(there are always empty seats
beside us).

"Pull up a chair, boys!
Join the party."

Levi shoves a chair out
with his Doc Martens boot,
like a cowboy
at a saloon
in an old Western.

I'll say this for him:
he never gives up
trying
to make me some
friends.
I'll even admit
that it's working
with the kids
in my pod
in Language Arts,
who have just started
getting my jokes
that Levi repeats.

The cafeteria boys
hover uncertainly,
turning away,
scanning the room,

conferring,
deciding,
unsure.

We see them
swoop in
with mannerless haste
to grab the table
the second we
leave.

                              "Rude,"

mutters Levi,
with a quick
protective glance
at me,
as if I
actually
cared.

DISGUISE

"I have something to do," I say.
"You go have *your* lunch."

                              "Oooh, big secrets?"

Levi winks,
which is so annoying
because
my errand,
my *mission*
is not winkable.
It is
        important,
        urgent and
        deadly
        serious.

But at least he leaves.
He never seems to need
privacy
but at least he understands
that I do.

I turn and steer
down the clear
empty halls
of the school —
a gliding ghost.

                              All the way
                        to the back
                  over by the gym
                  down a hall
            lined with benches
            leading to a door
      to the parking lot

and the football field.
That's where I'll find Carter,
and maybe learn more
of his secrets.

I'm there first.
I park
near the door, looking out
like I'm waiting for someone —
then,
like all good spies,
I assume a disguise:
tilt my head to the side,
and let my body

        crumple

                a

      little

            bit

                    more.

And, like magic,
even when random kids
pass by,
when Carter
and his gang
burst through the doors
in a cloud of vape smoke
and body spray
and collapse on a nearby bench,
none of them —
        not one of them —
    sees me at all.

                Invisibility
              is my superpower.

THE MEASURE OF A MAN

I've watched Carter
for three months,
since he got that first
undeserving gift
of Daria's smile
and my blood
ran
cold.
I've tracked him
with

       firm resolve,
       cunning stealth
       and
       steely determination.

And now I know him.

He wields his
power
with a flick of his
shaggy brown hair,
a sly smile,
a sarcastic comment
and his aura of
lawless
recklessness.
He rides
effortlessly
on the strong waves
of his popularity.
There's never an empty seat
beside *him*.

Crowds part
for him
for a different reason
than they do
for me.

I've heard him
laugh
about cheating
on exams
and girlfriends.
I've heard him
boast
about stealing
from the corner store,
and more —

                                        "This fountain pen?"

He twirled it in his hand
showing his friends.

                                        "From the principal's office."

I would have left him alone,
none of this would have begun
if he hadn't
turned his stare —
his hot glare —
on innocent
Daria.

But he did, and
        because I'm bound to protect her,
        because I've taken his measure,
            and found him
            unworthy,
                he can only blame
                himself.

NOWHERE NEAR NOBLE

At first,
I merely observed him.
I watched him
       flirt
       with any girl in range,
              bully
              other students
              (sometimes subtly,
              often mercilessly)
                     and ridicule
                     the staff
                     behind their backs
                     (or even to their faces).
The kindly,
elderly
custodian
is his favorite target.
I can only imagine
what he'd say
about my mother.

He also
enthusiastically,
wickedly,
ironically
high-fives the
school constable,
because his contempt for the law
is so very funny.

So far,
he's left me alone.

Not out of
decency
or — worse —
pity.
Utter lack of interest
is one of his crimes.

How can I
describe the depths of his
ignorance?
He would be *shocked* to
discover that I
exist at all,
that I'm actually a
human being,
let alone one
with an intelligence
keener than his own,
and a far
nobler
heart.

He's even worse
than the familiar type,
who sees only
the chair,
some bony limbs,
a crumpled lump,
                    period.

If I was pointed out,
he would
describe me in
crude,
hateful,
predictable words

that would say far more
about him
than
they ever
could
about
me.

NOBODY

I got my first clue
that something
unusual
was afoot
last Wednesday.
It was the
same time,
same place,
but Carter
was different.

Keyed up
           excited
   buoyant
         dangerous
               as a
        coiling
              snake.

He looked up
and down the hall,
looked right at me,
right through me,
and said:

                "Good.
                Nobody's around."

FLY ON THE WALL

But Fly was right there,
cunningly,
openly invisible,
disguised as Nobody,
as Nothing.
Fly in the hall,
a fly on the wall —
        watching,
        listening,
        missing nothing,
        remembering.

I have keen
hearing and
can even lip-read a bit.
A useful skill
that brilliant
Edward from the
special class
in sixth grade taught me —
speech made visible,
every last syllable
(certain swear words,
in particular,
are not hard to spot).

"So: wanna make some money?"

Carter asks his friends.

"*Serious* money.
My cousin
told me all about it.
So I'm telling you."

And you're telling me, too,
Carter.
You're
telling me
all about it.
And you don't
even
know it.

"You in?"

Carter asks his friends,
sitting back,
confident already
that they were,
not needing
nervous nods to
know it.

I'm in, too, Carter,
I vow.
"Nobody" is in.

T[ST OF [NDURANC[

"I want you to try this,"

my mother says,
slapping down a pamphlet
like a challenge.

"It's at the center where you
do physio.
Aqua therapy!
Exercise in a *pool*!"

"In water?" I ask
blankly,
which of course it is.

She reads out the
long list of benefits
this hydro-torture
promises:
    muscle tone,
        strengthened bones,
    coordination,
        circulation,
            relaxation,
    ability,
        stability,
            flexibility
(or so says the pamphlet).

Also, she reads,
looking at me
meaningfully,

"It improves
self-esteem"

(as though flailing in water
to keep from going under
will somehow
make me feel better
about myself).

"I hate water."

"It's been *years*, Felix.
You were six!"

"I almost drowned!"

"Gulped a little water down."

"Pass."

"I've signed you up."

"*No way.*"

"You start Saturday."

"*Not. Interested.*"

Final.
Definite.
Loud.
Couldn't be clearer.

"Tyrell is going, too.
It'll be fun."

Seething,
I glance at the
loathsome pamphlet
as she makes dinner.

All kids love swimming!
it begins.

Loaded,
daring anybody to
argue
with pure,
simple
childhood fun.
My heart sinks
like a
stone,
as I imagine
sinking like a stone
in deep
        deep
            water.

Because I am
powerless,
yet again.
And because
this waterlogged
flail-fest,
like lots of things,
starts with a lie.

QUEST

That night,
as the television screams
in the next room,
I focus.
And put my plan into
action.

Tablet secured,
pointer Velcro-strapped
to my steady left hand,
I pause.
(There are other technologies
Levi is always urging on me,
but I like
using my pointer —
typing
like everybody else.
A ten-inch screen
and an alphabet
hold a whole world
of freedom).

First, an account.
Quixote? Too revealing.
DQ1605? Unappealing.
I settle on
knightwatch@ringmail.com.
It has a nice ring:
dignified,
true
(even, possibly, cool).

Letter
        by letter
                by letter

    I tap.

Patience
has become
one of my virtues.

> *I know what*
> *you're doing.*
> *— Nobody*

That's all.
Short and sweet.
Simple.
Cryptic.
That's the strategy for Carter.
Rattle him.
Hint.
Get under his skin.
I press "send"
before I'm tempted to add
more.

ONE MORE

And then another
message.
Completely,
totally
different.
The thought
of her
reading it
makes
my heart
      thud,
           and my hands
            grow
               cold.

I take a ridiculous
number of tries
and agonize
about how
to appear
to Daria.

I finally type:

> *Carter is a danger.*
> *You should feel safer*
> *knowing I am watching out for you.*
> *— A friend*

I memorized their emails
from the list that came around
in Health last term,
so Mr. Day could send us

important information
on carbohydrates,
diseases,
drugs
and personal space.
I figure
this is at least as important.

I press "send"
just before
my mother comes into the kitchen
and tells me,

                        "Show's almost on, kiddo."

She pats me on the shoulder,
flips through *Don Quixote*,
smiles,
reaches for a bag of chips
and asks me about
the homework
I never did.

ANCESTRY

I worry about my mother's
aching arms and legs
and the extra burden
for her
of me —
she's four years
from sixty,
and honestly,
she looks older.

I think of her
when I wait for the bus,
and see
other kids' parents:
        yoga moms,
            bro-dads,
      business-suited types,
          far younger,
      who run marathons,
          host dinner parties,
      take weekend trips,
          herd younger siblings
      and drive
          bucket-list cars.

But while Mom's
life is hard
she's young at heart
with a ready smile
trembling into a
hearty laugh
at the slightest
joke.

I don't remember
my father,
who was even older
than my mother.
He died suddenly
when I was three

                              "Because his heart was always
                              too *big*,"

Mom says,
leaving only his picture
up there on the wall,
and a name —
Stanley Landon Yarrow
(SLY!
Way cooler than FLY) —
scratched in
spidery handwriting
in a few books,
including my *Don Quixote*.

White-haired, bearded,
I think he looks like a
Russian poet.

                              "Santa Claus! He's a dead ringer!"

Mom says.
But in the photo
he's serious,
even stern,
definitely no jolly twinkle in that eye.

I wonder what
my father thought
of Don Quixote.

I seek clues,
flip pages,
searching for
the occasional note
or
special sentence
underlined in faded
pencil.
Like:

> *I know who I am*
> *and who I may be*
> *if I choose.*

Did his too-big heart
also thrill
and
swell
with those words,
with the ideas of honor
and courage,
as mine does?
I like to think
DQ's a link,
a bond
between
us.

GREEN

Levi wasn't kidding
about the green smoothie,
unfortunately.

"Kale, spinach,
almond milk and
protein powder,
num, num, num!"

He stirs the
alarming,
thick,
revolting sludge
with a
sturdy straw.

He's gone to a lot of
trouble
and I know,
with a
sinking heart,
that I'm going to have to drink it.

It tastes like
ground bark
(or just *ground*),
but I dutifully
choke it down.
I'm touched
by the gesture,
by this "meal" he's made;
he's an aide —
he's paid
whether I
eat
or not.

I brace myself, and
take another
brave,
determined sip.
"It's good," I lie,
gagging it back,
certain my teeth are
slimy green
like the napkin
he's using to
wipe my face
clean.

"Success!
Triumph!
Victory!"

he crows loudly,
dramatically.

"I'll make you another one
tomorrow!"

REACTION

Is it my imagination
or is Carter
jumpy today,
the day after my
message?
A quick,
searching
scan
of the hall,
a darting glance
over his shoulder,
makes me think
that
he is.

He's cranky, too.
Irritable,
impatient,
angry,
a dragon
scorching everything
in his path.
Everything except
Daria.

A small incident,
seemingly
unimportant,
strengthens my resolve.

As Daria and her friends
pass Carter's trio,
he reaches out
and pulls the

binder from her hand.
She shrieks,
laughs,
pleads for its return.

He
                        darts

            ducks
                                    hides

        then finally
            gives it back,
                hand
                        meeting
                            hand.

It's a silly episode.
Trivial.
Run-of-the-mill
school
hallway
stuff.
Meaningless.

But I shake
with fear,
worry,
helplessness,
and blindly
turn my chair
and steer
elsewhere.

        Anywhere
                elsewhere.

ROGUES

Something
was supposed to happen
today.
Friday.

           "The drop,"

Carter
called it,
ominously,
on Wednesday.
The *Drop*.
    Of *what*?
          From *whom*?
       For whom?
        How?
          And *where?*

I need to know,
so here I sit.
Fly in the hall,
doubly invisible,
shielded by
earnest students
painting a long
anti-bullying banner
(perfect cover).
     Waiting.
     Watching.
     Alert.

          "There he is."

My trio tenses,
peering out the far door.
Two of them are
uncertain, and

scramble to their feet.

"Stay here,"

Carter orders,
pointing down
like they're dogs.

Sit.

Stay.

He thrums with
energy,
anticipation,
excitement.
This can't be a good sign.
It must,
in fact,
be very, very
bad.
A predator
on high alert.

Elaborately
casual,
he looks around and,
seeing Nobody,
shoves his hands in
jean pockets and
slips through the door.

A black car outside,
low, curved and
beetle shiny.
Dark windows,
dirt-smeared
license plate.
I wish —
for the first time
in my whole life —

that I was a car-guy
so I could guess
the make.

I don't know
much
about what's happening,
but I *do* know
that when the car pulls away,
when Carter comes back,
in a gust of
exhilaration,
his eyes are dancing
and he's shoving something into
the pocket of his hoodie.

                        A successful

                               kill.

THE ART OF LANGUAGE

For some reason
(probably Stephen Hawking,
who — *news flash!* —
didn't have the same disability
as me),
once people understand
the basic fact
that my intelligence is fine,
they assume
that I must be
good at
math.

It annoys me that I am.

Numbers are
pure,
uncomplicated,
an escape,
a relief,
a distraction.
There's no
people messiness
with
numbers.

But still,
my favorite class
is Language Arts.
We sit in pods of four,
and my
quartet
is a lively one.

Gradually,
       incrementally,
             slowly,
                slowly,
                   slowly
I'm starting to relax.

The others are, too.
That dreaded
silent
embarrassment,
over-politeness,
discomfort leading to
avoidance
of the weird kid
is mercifully
evaporating.

For example,
Maddie
(of whom I'm wary,
who's louder than Levi
and tough and scary)
laughed
at my sarcastic joke
(not just politely,
because she's not polite.
It was a helpless,
yelping,
gum-showing laugh).

Anya doodles
cunning caricatures,
and she finally
did one of me!

There I am,
    narrowed eyes
        looking sideways,
            fly wings sprouting
                from shoulders,
                    open book in hand,
                        a speech bubble there
                            near my nose in the air,
                            saying:
                                "You are all so *childish*!"

Nailed it.

Carlos doesn't say much
but he laughs a lot,
and shares his gum
(that I can't have,
for fear of choking,
but that's not the point),
and his stuff
slides halfway
across my desk,
which I don't mind at all.
It's the sort of
casual thing
friends might do.

Sometimes
the tiniest things —
a gummy giggle,
a rude doodle,
the snap of shared gum —
are enough.

THE LAW

Later, Levi and I
hear a familiar voice.

"Fly-Guy!"

It's Constable Mah,
school "resource officer,"
a cheerful cop,
raising his hand
for Levi's high five.
Constantly high-fiving,
chatty,
casual,
he sails
back and forth
from our school
to the one next door,
happily oblivious
of any bad behavior.

Even with his
shiny black boots,
uniform and
assorted weaponry
he's hardly an
imposing
guardian of the law.

"How's it going, Buddy Boy?
All good?"

Constable Mah's
dignified nicknames for me
include such zingers as

"Little Dude,"
"Big Fella,"
"High Roller,"
"Whiz-Kid,"
"Buckaroo"

and,
wait for it,

"Dr. Awesome."

His eyes start on me
then wander over to Levi
for the answer,
like we're a package deal,
a two-headed beast
with only one head that
really speaks.
But he pats my shoulder
because he means well
and assumes we're
awesome
buddies.

COMMUNICATION GAP

"You should get a pair of purple pants
like Levi,"
I say
with a straight face.
It's beneath me, but
I mess with Mah
because he never,

       ever,

          ever
understands what I say.

                "Ah."
Constable Mah smiles,
nods,
not understanding.

                "Haha. Good, good."

I don't blame him.
Despite endless
speech therapy
(since I was *three*)
many people don't understand me.
My own mother often doesn't.
My frustrating mouth,
clenched teeth
and uncooperative tongue
block my thoughts
on their way out,
like a boulder
stopping a stream.

You have to concentrate.
Fixate.

Isolate
sounds and syllables.
Translate
what I say
into what I'm trying to say.
Patience
is a virtue
many people lack.

"Look, you can't entirely
blame the guy.
There are some cool new
voice technologies
we could try ..."

said Levi
weeks ago.
(But I figure
since I have a voice
I'd like to use it
rather than having
some robot
voice my thoughts.)

I *do*, however,
blame
Constable Mah
for not admitting
he doesn't understand,
for faking it,
for smiling
and nodding
away a
real conversation.

That's why I mess with him
but always,
afterward,
feel a little mean.

"What was that about my
purple pants?"

laughs Levi,
shaking his head.

"Better than last time
when you told him
the gym was on fire.
Freaked *me* out."

I'd been frustrated,
aggravated,
wanting to shock.

"Ah, haha,"

Constable Mah had
chortled,
        smiled
            and nodded.

"Good, good."

I do wonder what Mah
would say if I told him
right here
right now
what I suspect about Carter?
Because despite what he might say,
it's not
        ah,
        haha,
        good,
        good.

DREAD DEPTHS

"Dude, *you're* here?
At the *pool?*"

It's Tedious Tyrrell.
Dr. Obvious.
My supposed friend.

"Looks like it," I say,
and he laughs
because that was,
of course,
utterly
hilarious.
Tyrrell smiles a lot,
laughs a lot.
Too much,
in my opinion.
But everybody likes him.

"A real charmer,"
my mom says.

"Total sweetie."

Not
                prickly,
            difficult
        and
      sarcastic,
like me.

All we have in common,
as far as I can see,
is our disability
and even in that
we differ —

mine is
more "profound"
(translation: worse).
But somehow
that one thing
is
everything.
And
because of it
everyone
expects us to be
great friends.

Random question:
Do we assume
the same
commonalities for
           redheads?

                           boys with size nine feet?
                 girls who are five foot three?
                       left-handed people?

Would we be shocked
that in the end
they didn't become
just *awesome* friends?
You get my point.

Our mothers
watch from the stands;
I hear them   joking,
                 laughing,
                 talking,
                 visiting.
True friends.

My mother: short, stocky and pale.
His: tall, thin and dark.
One older, one younger,
one a single mom of a single son,
the other partnered in a family of five.
Nothing much in common,
other than having
kids
like
us.
Maybe that's enough
for them.
Or maybe they've
        discovered
                more.

I turn my attention to
the serious business
of not drowning.
My teeth chatter
with a bone-deep
cold after the
lukewarm
splash
in the showers.
The pool,
the building,
everything
is
                        fuzzy

                                dreamlike

            disorienting

without my glasses.

"Wow! It's deep!"

Tyrrell offers
this killer insight
as we steer our chairs
to stare
down into the
fathomless depths.
All that's missing from this
nightmarish
watery abyss
are circling sharks.

"Hope we don't drown, man!"

laughs Tyrrell,
smacking my shoulder.
He echoes my thoughts,
and cold dread
trickles down my spine.
I cannot imagine
how this
bad dream
could
possibly
help my
self-esteem
or anything else.

"Felix? Ready for some
splash-therapy?"

Everyone's a joker, it seems.
The wet-suited therapist
seems far too small
for
    hauling
    waterlogged bodies,

administering
basic
lifesaving
maneuvers
            or performing
            energetic CPR.

But at least she
wrestles me into a
life jacket
before she straps me
into a lift
and lowers me
            like
            dangling
            bait
into the
            waving
        waiting
            water.

SEA CREATURE

The warm water
swallows me up,
all but my head,
which,
mercifully,
stays afloat.

My frustrating body
predictably
        struggles
            and flails —
   thrashing
       in the crashing waves
          I'm causing.

                "Aaand, *relax*, Felix."
She pushes a pool noodle
under my arms.
                "Just float for a while."

And the terror of leaving my chair,
of being heaved in the air
and dropped
like a stone,
dissolves
in the warm,
soothing water.

For timeless
peaceful
moments

my body
unclenches,
rides the waves
of Tyrrell's entry
and stills.

Weightless,
   light,
     buoyant,
       jubilant,
an aquatic-themed
    flying dream,
       floating

        free,

          free,

           free.

REPLY TO A REPLY

I come home a
weary,
shaky,
heavy,
wheeled
land animal.
But the feeling of floating
lingers
like a catchy song
running through my mind.
I'm more than willing
to do some exercises to earn
that feeling again.

"See?"

says Mom.
I don't say anything, but
she knows me
so well.

"Admit it. You had fun,
you little fish."

She natters on.

"New adventures,"

she says, pointing at
Don Quixote.

"Just like that guy!"

So misguided
to equate DQ's
solemn quests
with a dip in a pool,

I think,
but
I let her talk,
let her enjoy her
little victory.

I flick on my tablet, and
what's this?
A reply to my email!
Unexpected.
I anticipated
simmering,
      surly
         silence.

My steady left hand
even shakes
as I open
Carter's first-ever
communication
with this Nobody.

> *You know nothing*
> *you pathetic loser.*

Carter writes
eloquently.
And adds two more
predictable words
I've edited
out here.

Charming, isn't he?

He deserves another:

You thought
today's drop
was secret.
You were wrong.
— Nobody

MIGHTY STEED

In the dark
depths
of the night
I lie awake,
sometimes for hours,
trapped on my back
by my
traitor body,
not wanting to wake Mom
to turn me over.

Lying,
    staring at the far wall
        with the crack
            that snakes down
                behind the painting of
                    the brown horse
                        that my mother bought
                            at a thrift shop
                                when I was four
                                    and wild about horses.

It's a crude painting,
amateurish,
someone just learning
perspective.
A too-short neck,
too-long legs,
the face of a
camel?
A moose?
Possibly hoofed.
Certainly not a horse.

The mane and tail ripple
horizontally,
even though it's
motionless,
and there's no wind
fluttering the leaves
of the bush-like
trees.

But Rocinante
(my mother misheard
the name
of Don Quixote's horse
and calls *him*,
absurdly,
"Rosie")
is as much a part of my room
as the Spain-shaped
stain on the ceiling.

He appears in my dreams
sometimes.
Perfected —
a glorious,
glossy,
gleaming steed,
muscular,
powerful,
mane and tail rippling in the
strong,
true wind.

I sit calmly in the saddle,
the sun on my face,
and

with the merest
twitch
of the reins
in my steady left hand,
we thunder off
on dignified,
unspecified
quests.

ADULT SUPERVISION

Why don't I tell
someone,
anyone,
what I suspect
about Carter,
you ask?
The principal,
Constable Mah,
Levi
or even my mother?
I've considered and
rejected
each of them in turn.

I might say it's because
I have no real proof
(so far)
of
Carter's crimes.
Only what I've heard
and my suspicions
based on
observations.

But the truth is,
this plan,
this quest,
is completely,
utterly
mine.
It gives me purpose,
focus.

There are no
dreary,
depressing
days
on the hunt.

I'm not ready,
yet,
to let an
adult in
to ruin
the
game.

WORTHY ADVERSARY

The Carter situation
requires
infinite patience,
toughness,
on-the-ground
intelligence.
A fly on the wall.
This FLY on the wall.

If I'm honest with myself,
I'm in too deep
to stop.
How could I leave
protecting Daria,
pursuing Carter
to someone else?
I couldn't.

I don't want to.

I confess
that
sometimes
the rush of power
I feel
when I hit "send"
alarms me.

But when I watch him
like a hawk
the next day,

and detect
    irritability
        watchfulness
  aggression
    or anger,

I feel a
  deep and
    secret
      satisfaction.

And my resolve is
strengthened,
like the blade of a sword
forged in fire.

CHARMING

Carter plays it well,
the charmer
with a ready smile,
a skillfully drawn
mask.
But I know him.
I don't underestimate
him
as he underestimates
me.

I've seen his flash of rage
quickly hidden.
Heard his comments —

                        cutting,
                        crude,
                        rude,

taunting words tossed
casually
like darts,
uncaring that
people still bleed
from
tiny holes.

He is a laugh
at someone else's
expense,
a bulging hoodie pocket,
a roll of bills
flashed
to impress.

And here I sit —
his
     unlikely,
          invisible,
               watchful
                    enemy,
                         silently
                              readying
                                   for
                                        battle.

REVELATION

Tyrrell is lifted,

                shifted,

    lowered

    inch

    by

    inch
into the pool.

Four sessions in,
and the cameras
roll as
a crew shoots
a short film on
aqua therapy.
(I locked my wheels,
refusing
a starring role.
I'd rather
literally
be shot.)

Laughing,
    joking,
        shrieking,
Tyrrell seems delighted.

He
    splashes,
        thrashes
on cue.

He does exactly
what they want him to do.

He dutifully
tells the interviewer
the pool is
                              "fantastic!"

The nice therapist says he's
                              "awesome!"
(that word again)
and has made
                              "amazing progress!"

which is not apparent
to me.

I watch from my chair,
as Tyrrell performs
an encore
and
suddenly
I understand him
just a
little
bit
more.

We *do* have something in common,
I realize:
        we're both
        in the same game,
                both judged by
                a jury of our peers,
                        and every day
                        we're on display.

Are we what they want us to be?
Are we enough?

Here's how it goes:
if you're not
a prodigy,
you're just an oddity.
If you aren't
impossibly intelligent,
superhumanly brave,
awesomely inspiring
(or whatever else they need),
what use are you?

How do they even compute you?

Average is not an option.

Was it the same for old DQ?
Did others call him crazy
because it was
scarier
if he was
right
in his fight
against injustice,
and the
rest of the world
was wrong?

Maybe those of us on the
outside
see more clearly
looking in.

The crew leaves
and the pool is safe.
"Great job, Tyrrell,"
I say, kindly,
as I'm lowered in
beside him.

                    "Thanks, man!"
he laughs,
and splashes water in my face.
                    "Watch me on the news tonight!"

And I see
his relief
that he was just what they
needed him to be.
    Brave.
    Happy.
    Inspirational.
    Incredible.
        Awesome.

ANY ANIMAL

"If you could be
any animal,"

says Levi
loudly
in the hall
before class,

"what would you be?
Other than a fly."

He is in his
          random
               perky
   chatty
                    hyper
         exhausting
mood,
which I dread.
He could ask anything,
talk about anything,
tell me
literally
anything.

I close my eyes.
My last aide,
Sami,
did the job
without
almost any
conversation at all.
It wasn't
optimal.

"Sami the Slacker,"
Mom called him,
but being
ignored
and bored
by Silent Sami
had its advantages.

Today,
I am in no mood
for this
mindless,
            useless
                    chatter.
I am planning,
plotting
a dangerous course.
I need my wits
about me.

I won't pick an animal.
I will *not*
encourage,
prolong,
condone
this childish
conversation.

As I stay silent,
face turned away,
he nudges me
theatrically.

"Hellllooo ...
anybody home?
Come on, what animal?"

I flinch away.
"Grow up," I hiss
with a
withering glance.
"Would you just *grow up?*"

Levi flushes,
backs up,
closes up,
gets up,
walks away and
tosses

                                        "You can be a real jerk, Fly"

over his shoulder.

And he's right.
It's our first fight.

ANY ANIMAL (TAKE TWO)

At lunch
Levi offers food
(which I refuse)
without speaking
or looking
into my eyes.

His eyes are
stranger-hard,
his mouth set.
He is an
older
serious
stranger.

At break,
after he helps me,
he walks off
(without bouncing)
even before
I ask to have some time
alone.
By myself
in the crowded hall,
I tell myself I don't mind,
I'm used to being alone,
I could use a little
peace and quiet.
And I battle
guilt
valiantly
by trying to convince myself
that I was right.

But,

    green smoothies
    and offers of coffee
    and cheerful chatter
    and companionship
    and a thousand other
    Levi things
argue back,
and parry my thrust.

DQ wouldn't have acted
so unjustly,
a cold voice inside me
whispers.
No matter how annoying
his sidekick was
(and Sancho Panza was
plenty annoying),
he rose above the fray,
noble even in adversity.

And suddenly a little peace
    isn't so important.
And suddenly winning
    isn't either.
And suddenly I worry
    that I've gone too far
    and stranger-Levi will be my
    aide from now on.
Or Silent Sami might return.
Or someone worse.

ANY ANIMAL (TAKE THREE)

"Okay, so I'm *sorry*,"
I say,
in the library
as he straps my
tablet pointer on.
I stumble over the
unfamiliar word
and not because of the
difficult *s.*
I sound
more belligerent
than apologetic.

                                    "Whatever,"

he says,
pulling out textbooks.

"Well, I *am*,"
I say loudly.
"Sorry."

     Silence

Then:

                                    "Grow up.
                                    That's what my dad says."

     Silence.
     He sighs.
     Shakes his head.

                                    "Maybe you're both right."

He looks defeated,
depleted.
All the Levi kicked out of him.
And somehow
his cartoon-chipmunk T-shirt
and friendship bracelets
make me feel
so
much
worse.

I have to fix
this
and I don't
know
how.

"Is your dad a jerk, too?"
I finally ask.

Levi bursts out laughing,
slants me a
glance.

                              "Kinda,"

he admits.

"Horse."

                              "What?"

"Horse. The animal.
I'd be a horse."

                              "Look, just forget it. It's over."

"Horse."

"Forget it, man."

"Horse."

I try to
playfully punch
his shoulder,
but awkwardly,
it lands
nowhere near.

But his face clears,
he turns to me,
and Levi's back.
It's almost too easy,
and I worry for him
in this world.

"I didn't know
you like horses!
My aunt has one.
Marigold.
We should get you up riding!
I'll bring the horse pictures
she sent with her
Christmas card!"

It's an amazing idea
he tosses out
so casually,
as if just anyone,
including me,
could ride a horse.

What would he have said if I'd chosen "bird"?

Suddenly, I feel
much older
than his twenty-four years.
More aware of
life's limitations
than its
possibilities.
"What animal would you be?"
I remember to ask back.

As Levi
agonizes
about whether he would be
        a peacock,
                a leopard,
                        a kangaroo
                                or a monkey
(giving lists of pros
and cons for each),
I imagine myself,
carelessly
chair-less,
confidently
competent
atop a gleaming
steed
(more "Rocinante" than "Marigold"),
and even conjure
up
a blazing sunset
        for us
                to ride
                        off
                                into.

BEWARE

In evening emails
to Daria
I allude
to Carter's rudeness,
his crudeness,
his crimes.
He's bragged of
stealing and
cheating
but what he's doing now
is surely worse.
I'll find out.

She deserves
                        to know
                to understand
            to see
        to believe
in his basic
dishonesty.

I try for a light touch.
I want so much
for her to
feel that
Knightwatch
is a friend.

Hitting "send"
always feels
like a
solemn
promise.

RATTLE AND SHAKE

People might be
interested
in how you're making
all that money.
— Nobody

It's harder
and
harder
to keep these emails
short
and cryptic.
The more I say,
the more I
want to say.

Because I now
know
the drop
was some kind of pill.
I heard the shake.
I've had enough
medication
to recognize that rattle,
the sound of pills
in a plastic bottle.

And now,
this week,
I've seen him
selling them
at school.

I worry
about the kids who are
buying them,
seeking a quick thrill,
an escape,
trusting *Carter*
to tell them what they are.

A
sharp
urgency is
added to
my
plan.

STRICKEN

From my post,
I see Carter
call out to
Daria.
She stops,
turns.
I silently will her to
                    keep walking,
                                keep walking.
She is
so innocent,
so unaware of danger,
so vulnerable.

She stops,
turns,
smiles at him
(that smile,
that *smile*).
Hand on her hip.
                                        "What do *you* want?"

she says.
(Is it my imagination
or are her eyes
wary?)

My heart stops,
just for a minute,
before a group of students
blocks my gaze.

I crane my neck,
the students pass,

and
cold
emptiness
settles in
on me
      as I see
        that Daria and Carter
            have both gone.

A TORCH IN THE DARKNESS

As I lie awake
night after night
I fight
to gain perspective.

All this work
expended on a jerk
like Carter
seems
futile.

But is it worthwhile?
I think of   Daria,
            dishonesty,
          unfairness,
       justice,
     truth.

And even though it's embarrassing
to think
in such old-fashioned
terms,
the bare fact is
true:

           villains deserve to be vanquished.

JUSTICE

"What is that ginormous
book
even about?"

Tyrrell
shouts,
pointing to *Don Quixote*.

We're double-parked
post-swim
waiting for our mothers.
He wants conversation,
I choose evasion
and pretend
I didn't hear.

Speech is such an effort
and I'm tired.
But he
speaks much
more fluidly
than me
and wants to talk.

"C'mon, Fly.
What's it *about*?"

I give him
the bare minimum
and sum it up in
one
hopefully final
word.

"Justice."

                                    "*Justice?* Like,
                                    the law?"

"More like in life."

                                    "Riigght. Like there's
                                    any justice there."

Unusual,
bitter,
biting
animosity
from
happy Tyrrell
ignites my curiosity.

"There has to be,"
I argue.
"There is."

                                    "There's not.
                                    Just look at us, man."

He stretches
shaking arms
wide,
slaps the armrest
of his chair.

                                    "And look at *them*."

His eyes swivel to
kids playing in the pool.

                                    "Call that
                                    justice?"

I am startled,
        rattled,
by his perception
        and the direction
that idle question
        went.

And for once,
as I'm whisked off
by my mother,
I want to talk to Tyrrell
further
and ask him
exactly
what he meant.

He misunderstood
(of course
he did).
I wasn't talking
guarantees,
equivalencies.
Still,
something
fills me with
                unease
            about
        the idea
of justice.

"There has to be," I whisper
to my ghostly reflection
in the window
as I'm driven home.

SOLITARY HAND

It's time.

I've waited,
    watched,
        wondered,
            pondered
and
    carefully
        crafted
            a case.

I need to
    meet him
        face-to-face.

It's my
turn to
show
that this fly
on the wall
actually,
uncharacteristically
brings
a sting.

Will he
finally
see me?

Anyone else
I'd give another chance,
a warning.

But is there
any room to barter
with Carter?
No.

He's taken
    so much
        from
    so many
        for
    so long
that now
    he must take
        the consequences.

Meet me tomorrow at noon.
Hallway by the gym.
I have proof.
Come alone.
— Nobody

PROOF

And I do
have proof.
That was not a lie.
I have all the notes
I made
when I should have been
listening in class.
Times.
Locations.
Word-for-word
recitations
of what I've heard.
Descriptions of what
I've seen.
Proof.

And I have the pill.

The one that came

               spinning

          along the floor

     rolling

        in a wide

            smooth arc,

settling behind
the back leg of
the third bench.

The pill that Carter and his
customer
couldn't find, despite
a frantic,
not-so-thorough
search.

Nobody knows it's there
but me.
My frustrating hands
refuse to collect it
but I check it
every
single
day.

And there it sits,
still,
lonely,
mercifully
missed
by the swooping
loop
of the custodian's broom,
forgotten
by everyone
but me.

A
    small,
    round,
    pink,
    loaded,
    crucial
        piece of evidence.
                Proof.

TIME AND PLACE

"You're quiet today, Fly,"

says Levi.

"Anything wrong?"

Only that I have to unmask
a cunning villain
single-handedly
at high noon
with nothing but
my wits,
my resolve and
a little
pink
pill,
Levi.

"I'm okay,"
I lie.

He looks
unconvinced.

"Hey! Totally forgot!
I brought those pics of
my aunt's horse,
Marigold!
And *her* horse friend,
Buttercup!
Those'll cheer you up.
Total beauts!
Now where did I …"

He pats his pockets,
rifles his bag
in consternation,

but I'm
barely registering
this conversation,
because
anticipation
and desperation
are
    making
           me
                sweat.

Eleven fifty-five.
It's almost
time.
I need
to get rid of Levi.
Now.

IMPERATIVES

It has to happen at noon
when Levi has his break,
when I can go
alone
(after school,
there is no altering
the schedule of
Crabby Vic and the
special bus.
It is as unchangeable
as the rising of the
sun,
or the movement
of the
tides).

So, noon it is.
Five minutes and
we meet —
       face-to-face,
       man-to-man.
Just him,
    the Somebody,
and me,
    the Nobody
he's never seen.

I *finally* get rid of Levi
by pretending that
I *really* want
to see those pictures
of Marigold the horse,

which must be in his coat

or car

or someplace

that's

    definitely

        not

            here.

HOW I ROLL

As I glide through the halls,
my left hand
steers steadily
while the
    cowardly
        rest of me
    starts
            to

            s
                h
                    a
                k
                    e.

DISHONORABLE

My mouth is dry
as I turn the
last corner
into the
lonely
hallway.

And freeze.

What I see
makes
my heart
stall, and
my hands turn
ice
cold.

Against specific
directions,
     flouting express
     instructions,
          against all
          codes
          of decency,
not one
but
three
of them
are waiting for me.

I should have known.

Why had I
ever expected
honor
among these
thieves?

ADVANCE OR RETREAT?

With a
suddenly
clammy hand,
I bring
my chair
to a
standstill.

For a beat,
clawing panic
makes me
consider
retreat.
They haven't seen me yet,
haven't guessed,
wouldn't even believe
that I'm
the
threat.

They wouldn't
know
if I suddenly
U-turned,
turning it all
over to Levi and
Constable Mah.
        I'm still
        invisible,
            still
           nothing,
              still
              nobody
              to them.

Lightning quick,
my brain
contemplates,
estimates and
calculates
possibilities.

Certain pain,
    degradation
    and humiliation
    weigh
    very,
    very
    heavily
    on one side
    of the equation.

                But on the other,
                courage,
                dignity
                and
                self-respect
                (uncomfortable,
                even annoying traits
                as Carter's wolf pack waits).

But fear,
but pain,
counters my inner
coward-voice.
Let it go.
Dangerous
to stay.
It won't make a difference
anyway.

Another voice answers.
But Daria.
But the sad,
deluded,
vulnerable
pill-buying kids.
But right
over
wrong.
But truth.
But justice.

I know my side.

AN OLD FRIEND

And
in my jumpy mind,
an unlikely ally
rallies,
ghostlike
in clattering armor,
and
glides
to my side.

Don Quixote,
the old knight himself,
rears his ancient,
      shaggy,
        addled
          head,
surveys the
hallway
battlefield
with a
steely gaze,
    pauses
        then
          whispers,
            "Charge!"

FLIP SIDE

An optimist
would call it
bravery.

         A pessimist
         would
         say
         madness.

Two sides
of the same
coin,
I'm starting
to realize.

         It's now
         or
         never.

It's now.

FINAL INDIGNITY

I muster
my courage,
and roll
slowly
toward the
tense trio.

They
sense movement,

      look up sharply
and,

      seeing me,

         looking right at me,

    relax.

               "Just *that*,"
Carter mutters,
looking away,
denying me
the dignity
of even
a pronoun.

Dismissing me
like I was
    nothing —
    negligible,
    a nuisance,
    an annoyance,
      barely even human.

The merest
fly
to be
swatted   away.

Despair
and rage
blot out fear
and bolster
my
resolve.

It is clearly
unthinkable
to him
that
    I
could be
the enemy who has
stalked him,
tracked him
tirelessly,
mercilessly,
successfully.

That
    I
could be
his
final,
worthy
adversary.

Underestimated,
        minimized,
                ignored
                        again,
                                even
                                        now,
                                                at
                                                        the
                                                                end
                                                                        of
                                                                                it
                                                                                        all.

SHOWDOWN

"Fly! I got those pictures!"

calls a loud,
cheerful voice
behind me.

Levi!
What?
I turn my head
to see him
trotting
down the hallway,
toward me,
toward *them,*
waving an envelope,
totally
oblivious to
    the
    crackling
    tension,
        the smell of
        danger,
            the whiff of
            catastrophe
                in the air.

Oh, god,
I suddenly
realize,
it's the horse pictures
he promised to show me
to cheer me up,
because I've been so quiet,
because I told him

horses
are my
favorite
animal!

But Carter's group
doesn't know that.
Unwittingly, Levi has
lobbed the word
pictures
like a grenade.
They jump to their feet
clearly assuming
those pictures
are the
promised proof.

The three
spring into action.

"Noon. Must be him,"

Carter mutters.

"There's our guy. He
must've taken pictures of me
at one of the drops.
Get them!
Get him!"

Carter whistles at his dogs,
both of them
                    bigger
              faster
          younger
       stronger
and meaner
than
my loyal

trusty
     hapless
          clueless
               animal-loving
                    sidekick.

BATTLE

"No, no, *GO!*"
I yell at Levi,
swinging my chair around
as they rush
past me
and grab him.
Kind, gentle
Levi,
who is
so surprised,
his eyes so wide,
that
I would have found his expression
funny
if I didn't fear his
death.

Carter snatches the envelope
while the others punch
Levi down
to the ground,
where it becomes
more
convenient
to kick him.

It's not the
first time
I've thought
                    a spear,
         a sword
      or a lance

would
come in
mighty handy.

But
having none at hand,
there's nothing I can do
but
    scream
           and
                charge
                        blindly
                                into

                                the

                                fray.

NO MERCY

I push my chair
to full throttle,
gallop
and ram
hard
into the nearest
leg
(sadly,
not Carter's).
A grunt of pain
is sheer
music
to my ears.

Energized,
I

                              flail
                        wildly
          and
              actually
                        land
                a random
                              sort-of punch
          with
                a random
                              sort-of fist.

In the scuffling
scrum,
an elbow swings

                                        back,

                        which connects
                        with my face,

which snaps my
head back,
which flings off
my glasses.

Searing pain
    screams,
    shooting
through my jaw
    like a
    hot,
    pulsing
    red
    light.

Levi curls on the floor,
protecting his head
from the
unexpected
assault.

I don't
recognize
my own
screaming voice
as,
blood pouring from my nose,
I swing my chair around
blindly
and ram
        again,

        again,

        again.

There is no mercy
in battle.

REINFORCEMENTS

As another
yell
echoes down the hall,
Carter grunts,

"Go, go!"

At the thud of heavy
running feet
the three
cowardly
vermin
retreat —
swearing

scrabbling

slithering

scattering
swarming

out the far door.

"What the hell?"
mutters a dazed,
wild-eyed,
wild-haired
Levi.

"What the *hell?*"
he repeats to an
out-of-breath
Constable Mah
who,

for once,
has
actually,
accidentally,
miraculously
stumbled upon
the scene
of
a
crime.

AFTERMATH

"Jeez, buddy,
jeez!"

Constable Mah
hauls a wincing Levi
to his feet.

"Was that Carter?
It was.
And Devon
and Bryson.
I saw them.
Holy cow! Fly!"

He recoils
at the blood
gushing down
my face.

"What kind of
jerks would hit
a kid like *Fly?*"

He mops
uselessly
at my streaming nose
with a
previously white
handkerchief,
doing little
but preventing
me from
breathing.

"Fly gave as good
as he got."

Loyal Levi
rushes,
dazed and wobbly,
to my defense.
He is
bruised,
     bowed,
          bloody,
but unbroken.

He gives me a long look
out of a
swelling,
blackened eye,
connecting the dots.
He's more perceptive
than I thought.

Or maybe,
I think with a shock,
Levi
might
actually know
more about life than
I do.

"I'm guessing those guys
didn't just really,
really
want to see some horse pictures,"

he says.

"Am I right, Fly?"

I can't help
but gargle-snort

a blood-bubbly
laugh,
imagining
the
vicious trio
staring
uncomprehendingly
at Marigold
the horse.

ALIVE

"Long story," I say.

                                    "Yeah, well,
                                    seeing as how I'm
                                    somehow
                                    sort of
                                    involved ..."

Levi says, rubbing
his aching ribs,
touching his split lip,

                                    "I'd be happy to
                                    hear it."

But I'm experiencing
a phenomenon
called "delayed reaction,"
I think.
My
            ears are ringing
                    heart hammering
            body shaking
        jaw throbbing
            blood running
                    from my nose
        into my mouth
            and trickling
            disgustingly
            down
            my
            throat.

                                    "Poor kid,"

Mah says to Levi,
picking up my glasses
(bent,
not broken!),
shaking his head,
patting my shoulder
sympathetically.

                                    "Poor kid."

He's wrong
once again.
Even actively
bleeding
(a curious
new sensation),
pity is the
last thing
I've ever needed.

And right now,
especially now,
he would
probably
be
shocked,
even appalled,
to hear
that
        this poor kid
            never felt
        so
                alive.

INTO THE SUNSET

A long afternoon
with an
   unsmiling,
      non-high-fiving,
         tight-lipped,
            all-business,
               unfamiliar
                  Constable Mah
asking questions,
taking statements,
reading my notes,
collecting the pink pill from its
hiding place,
was
deflating,
anticlimactic
and
plain *dull*,
after all the
excitement.

But
Because Mah's talking
to everyone,
at least
I know
that Daria and
Carter
will both
finally
learn the
   whole
      entire
         truth.

I am
sore and
weary.
Bleary.
Looking forward
to going home
and watching
blaring,
mindless
TV with my mother
who (I hope)
won't fuss
too much
about my
black eye,
swollen nose
and
all the bloodstains.

"Dangerous
to play a lone hand, Fly,"

Constable Mah warns
finally,
shaking his head
at me and Levi,
still the
two-headed
person.

"*He* planned the whole thing,
don't look at me,"

complains Levi,
pointing at me.
Mah's eyes
rest on me.
On me
alone.

"Guilty as charged,"
I articulate,
enunciate
and smile.

His eyebrows rise,
he sits back
and snorts a laugh,
hearing me,
fully,
completely,
actually *listening*
for possibly the
very
first
time.

"All right, shoo,
I got lots of work to do.
You —"

Mah points at me,
tries (and fails)
a stern
cop frown

"— just roll on outta here."

A small
exchange
that felt like
another victory.

NO WORDS

"Looks like I'm not getting
those pictures of Marigold back,"

laughs Levi
who is
delighted
with all the drama,
and proud
as a parent
of me.

He says my
new nickname
is
"Sherlock,"
and tells me
I played
detective

"like a total *boss*!"

He doesn't hold
anything against me.
Even his swollen eye
and possibly
fractured
ribs,
which he
has to get
checked out
at the hospital
on his way home.

I wonder if I
would have been
as generous if
our situations
were
reversed.
I hope so.

"You should've
let me help,"

he says.

"If I'd known,
I coulda ..."

he struggles,
gesturing,
then winces in pain.

You coulda ruined it,
I think.

"I coulda, you know, *helped.*
At least helped.
We have to *talk*
more."

You're right. It's true.
I nod,
because my
full heart
makes me
wordless,
and I don't
trust
my
untrustworthy
tongue

not to snarl
what I say
anyway.

But he understands
my silence,
nods
and curls up
on the library couch.

Good old Levi:
        not
        only a
        sidekick,
                not
                merely a
                necessary
                assistant,
                        not
                        just
                        an aide
                                after all.

UNSUNG HEROES

The bell rings,
and Levi and I both jump,
wince in pain
and scramble.
We have to go
this instant
because
nothing's changed —
even now,
after everything,
we know that
Crabby Vic
waits for no man.

And as the excitement
of the day
dies away,
old routines
rush in,
clamp down
and slam
adventure shut —
and I'm back
in my
familiar
cage.

So we hurry,
same as always,
through
the crowd of
jostling kids
who are
oblivious,

unaware
and uncaring
that Levi and I
are the
                victors,
        the
                noble ones,
        the
                heroes
                        of
                                this
                                        story.

UNBREAKABLE TRUTHS

Strangely,
after exclaiming

"My poor boy,
your poor *face!*"

my mother
took the bloodstains
totally in stride
and tried
to listen calmly
to an
                edited
            shortened
        sanitized
version
of the truth.

"Good for you, smart guy."

She nodded briskly.

"You were brave
to do that.
That Carter —
what a little *brat!*"

At that hilarious description
I wheezed
and squeezed out
a painful,
honking
laugh.

"And you.
Just like your father.
Always talking justice.
Always with the truth."

And then she said
something amazing:

"What's that quote?
Something like
truth
being stretched so
thin
but it's
unbreakable,
and it surfaces
above lies,
like oil floats
on water.
(I always liked that
oil and water bit)."

"Mom!" I gasped,
remembering that underlined
quote from none other
than *Don Quixote*.

She shrugged.

"What, you think I never
read a book?
Read that one years ago,
bits and pieces,
here and there
when I had time
(which wasn't often).
I like quotes like that.
I always underline them.
Bad habit."

She cackled a laugh.

"Used to make
your poor dad
so mad!"

TRIBUTE

The next day,
Daria
walks toward me,
    stalks toward me,
        straight-line focused,
           purposeful.
It must be me
she's come to see
because there's
nobody else in the hall.

Levi has
tactfully (for him)
slipped away
after giving me
a huge,
theatrical,
massively annoying
        WINK!
with his good eye
(which I ignored).

Mah told me
Devon and Bryson
blamed
Carter
for the whole altercation
and even showed
grudging admiration
for
"that kid in the chair."
Carter showed
only contempt,

I assume
(but don't care).

Daria must know
that Knightwatch
is me,
that Carter's been
suspended,
that
    she
        is
           finally
                safe.

My breathing comes
quickly,
shallowly,
as I
uselessly
clutch my book.
I hope my swollen nose
and black eye
lend me a
dashing
pirate look.

I realize,
too late,
that chivalry
is
far
easier
from
                        afar,

like gazing
at brilliant,

distant stars,
and I wonder,
suddenly,
if this was really
about her
or
about the
idea
of her.

Regardless,
here she is,
here it is:
the moment
when she finally sees me —
me,
as I really am —
and understands
all
I've
done.
     I don't need
     thanks.
          I don't want
          tears.
               I just hope I've
               settled all her fears.

                    "So, like, what is your *problem?*"
she demands loudly
instead.

I blink.
Her unexpected
anger
hits me
like a cold,
biting wind.
"I ... I" is all I can stammer
before
she rages on.

"All those cryptic messages,
'*I'm watching you,*'"

she air-quotes.

"All that scary
stalker-talk.
OMG, do you have
any idea
how much that
creeped
me
out?"

DISTRESS

I gawk at her
helplessly,
as the awful truth
dawns on me.
                    I'm astonished,
                ashamed,
            appalled,
        apologetic
that
I
could have been
the cause of her
distress.

While I adjust
to the clear fact
that
        she's
        not thankful,
                she's
                not grateful,
                        she's
                        nothing but angry,
and that I'm
to blame,
I still feel a
traitorous
rush
of exhilaration.

Because she's
looking right at me,
yelling *at* me.
At *me.*

As though I was
anyone,
a regular person,
someone
deserving of anger —
worth a yell.

SOUL BENEATH THE SKIN

"So just *stop* it,
okay?
I'm not, like,
helpless, you know.
I can take care of
myself."

As I try
to stammer out
my second "sorry"
of the week,
Daria half turns away
then turns back
with something more
to say.

"And here's a tip:
You want to be somebody's
friend?
Don't go all *stalker* on them.
That's no better than
Carter
(who, FYI,
I already *know*
is a total *jerk*).
That's not flattering.
That's not a compliment.
A person is more than
how they look.
Talk to them.
Have a
conversation."

The extent of my
hypocrisy
      washes
          over
             me.
How many times
have I thought the
same thing?
Wished the same thing?
That people would
talk to me,
understand me,
not glance and
judge
without a word …

She is so
completely
right.
And I never saw
what I was doing
that way,
her way,
until she yelled it at me.

REACH FOR THE STARS

"You're right,"
I say, pretty clearly.
"I'm sorry."
It isn't the time
for explanations,
justifications.

But,
        because I want her to stay,
                        because I want a chance
                        to understand this
                        angry stranger-girl
                        I thought I knew,
                                        because I don't want
                                        this to end,
I have to try.
"So," I say
desperately,
"want to have a
conversation?"

She got it
first time
because she was really
listening,
looking,
concentrating
on me.

She stood back,
her frown cleared,
her cheek dimpled,
that smile flashed,
and she laughed.

And just for a second,
the whole
world
          was perfect.

"No, I *don't*,"

she said,
eyes still sparkling,
trying to get that smile
under control.

"I have to get to band
practice.
And I'm still *mad* at you,
okay?
But you're learning.
Later."

LATER

"Later."
I repeat the word
as she sprints
away.
What started so dismally
didn't end so badly
and that half-promise
of "later"
gives me hope.

Later,
if she really means it,
I will actually,
possibly,
have a conversation
with Daria.
In spite of everything
(my plan,
the emails,
Carter's downfall)
    I don't have a
        clue
          what she's like
            at all.
I *do* know
that she's
more complicated
and perceptive
and prickly
than my
distressed damsel
who was never
Daria.

I U-turn,
thinking
of all the things
I thought I knew
and,
rolling slowly,
contemplate
what's left to do.
From my observations
of only one school,
there's not a shortage
of injustices.
But so many causes
make me pause
because they're
so
dauntingly
big.

Maybe the trick is
starting small.

Later,
I will answer
all Levi's questions,
and ask him a few in return.
I will drink another green smoothie
and look at those horse pictures
and consider
the previously
unimaginable:
actually,
truly
riding
a real, live
horse.

Possibly.

Later,
when he's back at school,
I'll roll past
Carter,
who
I won't call a
"nobody"
because I know what
nobody-ness feels like,
and nobody
deserves
that.
Will I give him a
sideways glance?
Another chance?

                    Possibly.

Later,
I will
try to remember
the depths
behind
Tyrrell's smiling,
splashing
facade,
and see if we can be the
friends our mothers
hope
we already are.

                    Possibly.

Later,
seeing as how I'm being
crazily optimistic,
I may even
try to see what's
behind the wall of

Crabby Vic's
intense,
appalling
crabbiness.
And not just loathe him
    in secret.

              Possibly.

    And
    then
    there's
        me.

Clearly,
my powers of observation
aren't so strong —
in fact,
I've been dead wrong
about
almost
everything.

And painful as it may be
to admit that
what I ask of others
applies to me,
it's only fair —

      less hearing
      more listening,
          less watching
          more seeing,
              less judgment
                period.

      (All easier said than done.)

But I
will *try*.
I'll possibly,
likely,
(let's be honest)
probably
      struggle,
      stumble,
      blunder,
          even
             fail.

But
still,
I will
look injustice
(and myself)
straight in the eye,
    and
       try
         and
           try
             and
               try
                 and
                  try.

ACKNOWLEDGEMENTS

I am grateful to many people who helped with this story.

Thanks to my editor Sarah Harvey for her skilled oversight, to my agent Hilary McMahon for her editorial comments and support in difficult times, and to sensitivity reader Danielle Seybold for her thoughtful suggestions and encouragement.

Thanks to Yasemin Uçar and Jennifer Grimbleby for the book's editing and layout, Andrew Dupuis for the beautiful cover design, and the whole team at Kids Can Press.

Thanks also to Christine Beliveau at Alberta Aids to Daily Living, the Glenrose Rehabilitation Hospital and the I CAN Centre for Assistive Technology for answering questions and pointing me to resources, and to Villamanta Legal Service in Australia for years ago giving me the opportunity to help advocate for clients with disabilities. I am also grateful for the assistance from the Alberta Foundation for the Arts during the writing of this story.

I am obliged to Miguel de Cervantes for his classic *Don Quixote* and hope he wouldn't have minded his ingenious gentleman from La Mancha making a cameo in this story when he was really needed.

Finally, always, thanks to my family — my impossible dream come true.